First published in Canada, the U.S, and the U.K. by Greystone Books in 2021
Text copyright © 2019 by Mei Zihan
Illustrations copyright © 2019 by Qin Leng
First published in 2019 in China by China Children's Press & Publication Group Co., Ltd
Translation copyright © 2021 by Yan Yan

21 22 23 24 25 5 4 3 2 1

Greystone Kids / Greystone Books Ltd.
greystonekids.com

An Aldana Libros book

Cataloging data available from Library and Archives Canada
ISBN 978-1-77164-731-1 (cloth)
ISBN 978-1-77164-732-8 (epub)

FSC
www.fsc.org
MIX
Paper from
responsible sources
FSC® C016973

English text design by Sara Gillingham Studio
The illustrations in this book were rendered in ink and watercolor.

Printed and bound in China by 1010 Printing International Ltd

Greystone Books gratefully acknowledges the Musqueam, Squamish,
and Tsleil-Waututh peoples on whose land our office is located.

Greystone Books thanks the Canada Council for the Arts, the British Columbia Arts Council,
the Province of British Columbia through the Book Publishing Tax Credit, and the Government
of Canada for supporting our publishing activities.

MEI ZIHAN · QIN LENG

TRANSLATED BY YAN YAN

New Year

AN ALDANA LIBROS BOOK

GREYSTONE KIDS

GREYSTONE BOOKS · VANCOUVER/BERKELEY

Every New Year's Eve, I miss my daughter.
My child has become an adult so quickly.

In France, she studies, she writes. Fluent in French now, she translates literary classics like Saint-Exupéry's *The Little Prince* and *Wind, Sand and Stars* into Chinese. And she reads in English, too, going so easily from one language to another. Merrily, she weaves her way through Paris's four seasons. She didn't come home last summer. Nor did she come this winter.

She should have come back to Beijing for Lunar New Year.

She could have spent Christmas abroad and still been home in
time for the Spring Festival.

It would have been perfect, the best of East and West.

Our home would have been livelier, more bustling.

I would have had an excuse to buy fireworks.

I could have seen her with her hands covering her ears as I carefully lit the fuse with an incense stick.

But I must remind myself of what a long journey it would be.
Even if she wanted to come home, she would have had to learn
to give up on the idea. Oh, the distance, the journey! Every time
I go to visit her, I feel anxious to be so high up in the sky. Past
the deserts of Mongolia, through the clouds of Russia, I finally
enter European airspace. The dark night and the bright day
rise and fall in a mere dozen hours.

My now grown-up child picks me up at the Charles de Gaulle Airport. She sees the expression on my ashen face that looks so bewildered by the sun and the moon.

It's not only how far the trip would be; I think she must also feel that she is a grown-up. She now belongs in the place where she lives.

She has married a Frenchman, Sylvain.
She shops for groceries and cooks their meals.

During the day, she strolls down the street outside her home.

At night she turns in to sleep on their bed. It won't do anymore
to be constantly running to Mother and Father's side. It would
make her feel as though she hasn't grown up, as though she
doesn't have what it takes to be independent, to live a life of her
own with her new husband.

After all, now she can stand at her own apartment window
and miss her faraway parents. Perhaps feeling nostalgic for
her innocent, funny childhood adds to the Frenchness of her
Parisian life. Perhaps she believes that this is a sign of her
maturity and that her parents' hearts should be at peace!

Daughter, I think you might be right after all!

But it's New Year's Eve and I still miss you.

I wonder what you and Sylvain are eating at the moment.

What are you craving this New Year's Eve? It makes me sad to think of you roasting a chicken and some potatoes for the two of you. No matter that you are a good cook — that meal is simply too meager. You've learned how to make dumplings, but that isn't enough.

I wish there were a lavish feast on the table in front of you. The feast is the hallmark of a New Year. It is a necessary ingredient for summoning joy and holiday spirit. The feast must begin with cold appetizers and end with spring rolls dipped in vinegar. There must be egg dumplings, tofu skin rolls, and spinach in a casserole.

Then our hearts' contentment drifts up with the steam from the casserole and all worries give way. But, Daughter, you have none of that there. That's why every New Year's Eve, I sit before such a billow of steam with my heart filled with thoughts of longing, of missing you!

When I come to see you in Paris at your home on Avenue Victor-Hugo, I watch you fervently cooking French dishes and Italian pasta. Though it saddens me to see you work so hard for such a simple meal, it also somehow puts my heart at ease. You really are all grown up. You are no longer a child in your home, in that land full of sundry flavors.

In your journey, you have learned to accept new things, acquire new choices and new excitements. You are no longer that madeleine lover in search of lost time. Under an unfamiliar tree, you pick a fruit which you cannot name and smile happily. You have grown to love French baguettes and cheeses. You eat Italian pizzas with relish, seemingly ready to offer a speech in their praise.

Daughter, that's the way! That's what growing up is all about! That's what it means to live a full, rich life. The sign over the door of your childhood home and our familiar dining table will be in your memories forever. But to be living at a distant address with your little dining table is a sign of your accomplishment. It's a necessary part of life. It's what makes me feel proud and honored when I think of you.

It is the same sort of pride and honor I felt when I passed Montaigne's bronze statue as I stepped onto your Sorbonne campus.

It's true. You are no longer that one-year-old baby who slept on the couch while the adults were watching the Spring Festival celebration on TV, wishing Ma Ji's crosstalk comedy would never end.

You are no longer that four-year-old child carrying the big bunny lantern your cousin gave you, careful to keep the candle alight on your way to your kindergarten.

You are no longer that seven-year-old hugging the big stuffed
bear that I bought you from the shop on Zhunhai Road,
staggering under its weight.

You are no longer that eighteen-year-old praying for a high college entrance exam score, who ran to Longhua Temple in a daze to burn incense for Guanyin.

Everything has changed. You sit before the window of your apartment on Avenue Victor-Hugo wondering what other French books you could translate and recite for the Chinese people, for me, for readers who want more than mere flat words on a page.

You are no longer what you called yourself, a kite floating in your north-facing classroom. Now your window faces south. The dawn's first light and the turquoise sky appear before you as you lean into its infinity.

But, Daughter, I still miss you. I almost dread
New Year's Eve when you call me in the middle
of our feast. In that delicate, still childlike voice,
you say, "Daddy, are you eating New Year's feast?
What dishes did you make?" I want to cry because
I know that you still miss spending the holiday at
home. You miss the crowded table filled with food,
the spring rolls and the casserole. Behind the veil
of steam, no one can see the tears in my heart.

Daughter, it's New Year's Eve. Make yourself a feast
and enjoy it with Sylvain. Happy New Year!